SandCastle 3

Homophones

# They're There in Their Boat

Mary Elizabeth Salzmann

ABDO
Publishing Company

Published by SandCastle™, an imprint of ABDO Publishing Company, 4940 Viking Drive, Edina, Minnesota 55435.
Copyright © 2002 by Abdo Consulting Group, Inc. International copyrights reserved in all countries. No part of this book may be reproduced in any form without written permission from the publisher. SandCastle™ is a trademark and logo of ABDO Publishing Company.
Printed in the United States.
Cover and interior photo credits: Artville, Digital Stock, Eyewire Images, PhotoDisc, Stockbyte

Library of Congress Cataloging-in-Publication Data

Salzmann, Mary Elizabeth, 1968-
  They're there in their boat / Mary Elizabeth Salzmann.
    p. cm. -- (Homophones)
  Includes index.
  Summary: Photographs and simple text introduce homophones, words that sound alike but are spelled differently and have different meanings.
  ISBN 1-57765-650-4
  1. English language--Homonyms--Juvenile literature. [1. English language--Homonyms.] I. Title. II. Series.

PE1595 .S27 2002
428.1--dc21
                                                                    2001053306

The SandCastle concept, content, and reading method have been reviewed and approved by a national advisory board including literacy specialists, librarians, elementary school teachers, early childhood education professionals, and parents.

## Let Us Know

After reading the book, SandCastle would like you to tell us your stories about reading. What is your favorite page? Was there something hard that you needed help with? Share the ups and downs of learning to read. We want to hear from you! To get posted on the ABDO Publishing Company Web site, send us email at:

**sandcastle@abdopub.com**

# About SandCastle™
## Nonfiction books for the beginning reader

- Basic concepts of phonics are incorporated with integrated language methods of reading instruction. Most words are short, and phrases, letter sounds, and word sounds are repeated.

- Book levels are based on the ATOS™ for Books formula. Other considerations for readability include the number of words in each sentence, the number of characters in each word, and word lists based on curriculum frameworks.

- Full-color photography reinforces word meanings and concepts.

- "Words I Can Read" list at the end of each book teaches basic elements of grammar, helps the reader recognize the words in the text, and builds vocabulary.

- Reading levels are indicated by the number of flags on the castle.

**SandCastle uses the following definitions for this series:**

- Homographs: words that are spelled the same but sound different and have different meanings. *Easy memory tip: "-graph"= same look*

- Homonyms: words that are spelled and sound the same but have different meanings. *Easy memory tip: "-nym"= same name*

- Homophones: words that sound alike but are spelled differently and have different meanings. *Easy memory tip: "-phone"= sound alike*

## Look for more SandCastle books in these three reading levels:

| **Level 1**<br>(one flag) | **Level 2**<br>(two flags) | **Level 3**<br>(three flags) |
|:---:|:---:|:---:|
|  |  |  |
| **Grades Pre-K to K**<br>5 or fewer words per page | **Grades K to 1**<br>5 to 10 words per page | **Grades 1 to 2**<br>10 to 15 words per page |

**they're**

they are

**there**

that place
or
a pronoun

**their**

belonging
to them

**Homophones** are words that sound alike but are spelled differently and have different meanings.

Gabe and Aaron love ice cream.

Vanilla is **their** favorite kind.

Garen and Earl are brothers.

They're playing in their front yard.

We have fun at the beach.

We run from here to there.

There are puppies sniffing my face.

They make me giggle.

Ray and his grandpa play a game on their computer.

**They're** making a lot of cookies for the school bake sale.

**There** are two girls playing on the tire swing.

They are sisters.

They have fun on Halloween.

They're wearing their costumes to a party.

Jackie runs to second base.

She hopes she will get there safely.

Marsha and Nancy read together.

Their book is very funny.

**They're** blowing out birthday candles.

It is a fun party.

They're going to school.

They get there on the bus.

Ned and Quint lie in **their** hammock and eat **their** apples.

**They're** riding a paddleboat on the lake.

Larry waves to his mom.

Dale finds Chicago on the globe.

His grandma lives there.

These kids are in the back seat.

Who is in the front seat?

(their dad)

# Words I Can Read

## Nouns

A noun is a person, place, or thing

apples (AP-uhlz) p. 18
bake sale
 (BAYK SAYL) p. 11
base (BAYSS) p. 14
beach (BEECH) p. 8
birthday (BURTH-day)
 p. 16
book (BUK) p. 15
brothers (BRUHTH-urz)
 p. 7
bus (BUHSS) p. 17
candles (KAN-duhlz)
 p. 16
computer
 (kuhm-PYOO-tur)
 p. 10
cookies (KUK-eez) p. 11
costumes
 (KOSS-toomz) p. 13
dad (DAD) p. 21
face (FAYSS) p. 9
fun (FUHN) pp. 8, 13

game (GAME) p. 10
girls (GURLZ) p. 12
globe (GLOHB) p. 20
grandma
 (GRAND-mah) p. 20
grandpa
 (GRAND-pah) p. 10
hammock (HAM-uhk)
 p. 18
here (HIHR) p. 8
homophones
 (HOME-uh-fonez)
 p. 5
ice cream
 (EYESS KREEM) p. 6
kids (KIDZ) p. 21
kind (KINDE) p. 6
lake (LAKE) p. 19
lot (LOT) p. 11
meanings (MEE-ningz)
 p. 5
mom (MOM) p. 19

paddleboat
 (PAD-uhl-bote) p. 19
party (PAR-tee)
 pp. 13, 16
place (PLAYSS) p. 4
pronoun (PROH-noun)
 p. 4
puppies (PUHP-eez)
 p. 9
school (SKOOL)
 pp. 11, 17
seat (SEET) p. 21
sisters (SISS-turz) p. 12
swing (SWING) p. 12
there (THAIR) pp. 4, 8
tire (TIRE) p. 12
vanilla (vuh-NIL-uh)
 p. 6
words (WURDZ) p. 5
yard (YARD) p. 7

# Proper Nouns

## A proper noun is the name of a person, place, or thing

**Aaron** (AIR-ruhn) p. 6

**Chicago** (shi-KAH-goh)
p. 20

**Dale** (DAYL) p. 20

**Earl** (URL) p. 7

**Gabe** (GAYB) p. 6

**Garen** (GAHR-uhn) p. 7

**Halloween**
(hal-oh-EEN) p. 13

**Jackie** (JAK-ee) p. 14

**Larry** (LAIR-ee) p. 19

**Marsha** (MARSH-uh)
p. 15

**Nancy** (NAN-see) p. 15

**Ned** (NED) p. 18

**Quint** (KWINT) p. 18

**Ray** (RAY) p. 10

# Pronouns

## A pronoun is a word that replaces a noun

**it** (IT) p. 16

**me** (MEE) p. 9

**she** (SHEE) p. 14

**there** (THAIR)
pp. 4, 9, 12

**them** (THEM) p. 4

**they** (THAY)
pp. 4, 9, 12, 13, 17

**we** (WEE) p. 8

**who** (HOO) p. 21

# Verbs

## A verb is an action or being word

**are** (AR)
pp. 4, 5, 7, 9, 12, 21

**belonging**
(bi-LONG-ing) p. 4

**blowing** (BLOH-ing)
p. 16

**eat** (EET) p. 18

**finds** (FINDEZ) p. 20

**get** (GET) pp. 14, 17

**giggle** (GIG-uhl) p. 9

**going** (GOH-ing) p. 17

**have** (HAV) pp. 5, 8, 13

**hopes** (HOPESS) p. 14

**is** (IZ) pp. 6, 15, 16, 21

**lie** (LYE) p. 18

**lives** (LIVZ) p. 20

**love** (LUHV) p. 6

**make** (MAKE) p. 9

**making** (MAKE-ing)
p. 11

**play** (PLAY) p. 10

**playing** (PLAY-ing)
pp. 7, 12

**read** (REED) p. 15

**riding** (RIDE-ing) p. 19

**run** (RUHN) p. 8

**runs** (RUHNZ) p. 14

**sniffing** (SNIF-ing) p. 9

**sound** (SOUND) p. 5

**spelled** (SPELD) p. 5

**waves** (WAYVZ) p. 19

**wearing** (WAIR-ing)
p. 13

**will** (WIL) p. 14

# Adjectives

An adjective describes something

**alike** (uh-LIKE) p. 5
**back** (BAK) p. 21
**different** (DIF-ur-uhnt) p. 5
**favorite** (FAY-vuh-rit) p. 6

**front** (FRUHNT) pp. 7, 21
**fun** (FUHN) p. 16
**funny** (FUH-nee) p. 15
**his** (HIZ) pp. 10, 19, 20
**my** (MYE) p. 9

**second** (SEK-uhnd) p. 14
**that** (THAT) p. 4
**their** (THAIR) pp. 4, 6, 7, 10, 13, 15, 18, 21
**these** (THEEZ) p. 21
**two** (TOO) p. 12

# Adverbs

An adverb tells how, when, or where something happens

**differently** (DIF-ur-uhnt-lee) p. 5
**out** (OUT) p. 16

**safely** (SAYF-lee) p. 14
**there** (THAIR) pp. 14, 17, 20

**together** (tuh-GETH-ur) p. 15
**very** (VER-ee) p. 15

# Contractions

A contraction is two words combined with an apostrophe

**they're** (THAIR) pp. 4, 7, 11, 13, 16, 17, 19